ESCAPE FROM
BLOOD CASTLE

Jenny Tyler

Designed and illustrated by
Graham Round

Cover design: Russell Punter

Contents

About this Book

Escape from Blood Castle is a mystery story with a difference. The difference is that you have to solve the mystery yourself.

The book consists of a series of puzzles, each of which must be solved for the next part of the story to make sense.

The story begins over the page. Just start reading. At the bottom of the page is a mystery to solve. Clues to the solution lurk in the picture and the words, so you will need to read, look and think carefully. Don't turn over until you have found the answer.

On later pages, the mystery sometimes relates to pictures and words you have already read. You will probably need to flick back through the book to look for clues.

If you get stuck, there are extra clues to help you on page 41. Find the section which refers to the page you are on and hold the page up to a mirror to read the clue. If you have to admit defeat, you will find all the answers on pages 42 to 48.

COUSIN BORIS

INTREPID IVOR

THE FRIENDLY SPIDER

THE MOUSE WHO HELPS IVOR

Intrepid Ivor and the Evil Baron

Ivor's heart thumped as he crouched, shivering, among the bushes. Looming in front of him was the object of his thoughts for many months – Blood Castle, home of the man Ivor knew as Cousin Boris, but who now refused to answer to anything but The Baron. Perhaps he should just turn round now and run home.

Ivor thought of his favourite TV heroes and pulled himself together. He couldn't let himself be cheated of wealth and title by his creepy cousin. His friends would never call him Intrepid Ivor again if he funked this.

Pausing only to check he still had his trusty survival kit in his pockets (useful things, such as chewing gum, pepper, nylon thread and half a chocolate bar), Intrepid Ivor made his way towards the castle's west wall, darting stealthily from bush to bush.

How to get in was the first problem. Ivor thoughtfully sucked his finger where it had caught on the sharp hook in his pocket and surveyed the scene in front of him. Suddenly he worked out what to do . . .

DON'T TURN THE PAGE YET.

This picture shows the building as Ivor saw it. How and where did Ivor get in?

GARGOYLES

SHARP SPIKES

POISONOUS LEAVES

YESTERDAY'S MILK

Inside Blood Castle

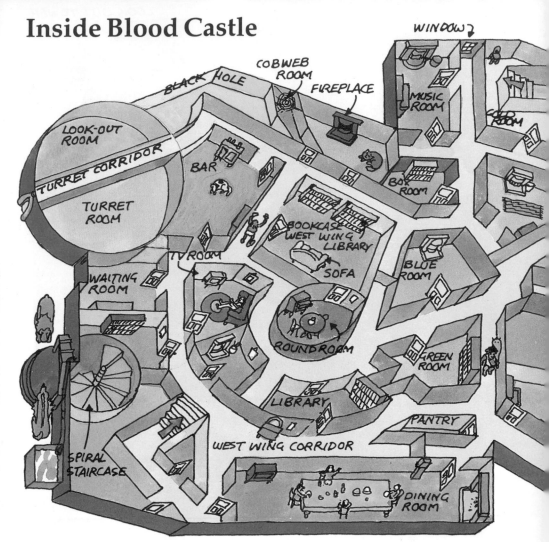

It was pitch black inside. Ivor shuffled along, feeling his way along the wall with his hand. He could see nothing – it was like walking blindfold. His ears strained for the slightest sound, but there was none.

He felt the corridor curve to the left and then turn sharp right. For a short distance the surface beneath his fingers became very smooth, but soon changed again to the same roughish texture as before. A dozen or so steps further on he felt the same temporary smoothness beneath his fingertips again. For the first time he could hear something. He paused. A faint snoring sort of sound reached his ears. He crept onwards – a slight left turn, followed by quite a sharp one and then a shaft of light.

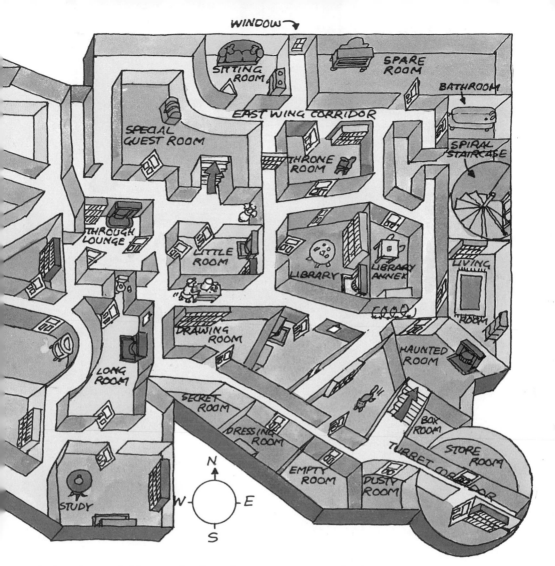

At last he could have a look at the map in his pocket and try to work out where he was.

Ivor's intention was to find the vital Papers which would show who was the rightful heir to Blood Castle. He had been told that they were in a room with two doors on adjacent walls and a fireplace on the wall opposite the larger door, with a large bookcase to its left.

DON'T TURN THE PAGE YET.

Above is a copy of the map Ivor carried in his pocket.
 Where is Ivor now?
 Which room should he go to and which route should he take to get there?

The Locked Door

BORIS

PEARL'S PIE

WASTE PAPER BASKET

AUNT MATILDA'S SPARE SPECTACLES

8

BELL PULL

MATILDA

UNCLE SPIKE'S WALKING STICKS

COAL BUCKET

FELIX

COLD TEA

With shaking hand, Ivor wedged the door open. Yes, there was the fireplace facing him with a bookcase to its left. It must be the right room. He opened the door a little wider and crept in.

A few steps took him to the middle of the room. Then his heart stopped as he heard a loud bang behind him, followed by the unmistakable sound of a key turning slowly in a rusty lock. He rushed to the door in a panic. It was indeed locked. The other door! Of course that was locked too.

As he frantically searched the room for a way out, Ivor almost forgot why he was there in the first place. The Papers! He might as well use his energy looking for them.

Nothing. In despair, Ivor sank down next to the bookcase and stared at the books.

''You've made a mess of this, Ivor,'' he thought to himself.

Suddenly he realized there was something very odd about the books. Picking a scrap of paper out of the waste-paper basket, he started scribbling furiously.

''Got it!'' he said aloud and jumped to his feet. In a few seconds he was out of the room.

DON'T TURN THE PAGE YET.

What did Ivor see and how did he get out of the room?

9

Another Map?

Ivor found himself in another room. He tried the door straight away. Whew! It wasn't locked.

He leaned against it, breathing a sigh of relief and realized, as he did so, that he still had in his hand the screwed-up scrap of paper he had been scribbling on. He was about to toss it away when he saw it had something on the back. He smoothed it out on the table and found that it was a map. It looked just like the one he had in his pocket. But was it really the same?

It took a minute or two for Ivor to check his heavily laden pockets, but eventually he found his own map, neatly folded up.

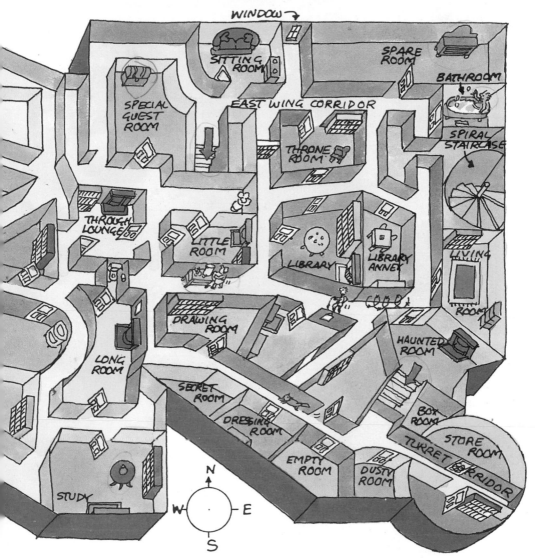

He compared the two maps very carefully. There were lots of tiny differences. Suddenly Ivor knew why he hadn't found the Papers – he'd been in the wrong room all the time. What's more, he knew what he had to do next.

Quickly snatching a useful-looking box from the table, he set off.

DON'T TURN THE PAGE.

This is the map Ivor found. Compare it with the one he had in his pocket (on pages 6-7) and see if you can find all the differences. How did Ivor know he'd been in the wrong room? Where did he set off to?

11

Ivor Meets the Tea Trolley

Feeling rather pleased with himself, Ivor quickly made his way to the stairs.

The noise was a shock. In his haste, he had forgotten that danger could be lurking round every corner. He thought it sounded a bit like crockery rattling, but decided he was being silly. It was obviously something much more sinister. It was getting louder too.

Suddenly all was quiet again. A friendly looking spider scuttled across the floor in front of him. Ivor enticed it into the little box he had in his hand. It made him feel better to have a friend – even if it was only a spider.

After waiting for what seemed like ages, Ivor spread himself round the corner at the top of the stairs. He was in an empty room. As he tip-toed out of the door and into the corridor, he could smell something which reminded him of strong, well-brewed tea.

Ivor crept along the corridors until eventually he spotted the source of the smell. There, all alone, was a tea trolley. A huge urn steamed gently among piles of the most delicious looking cakes and buns.

ARTHUR

FEL

PEARL'S FAVOURITE DRINK

SPIDER HOLE

GRANDFATHER BLOOD'S ARABIAN VASE

Ivor couldn't resist cakes and there didn't seem to be anyone about . . .
DON'T TURN THE PAGE YET.

Ivor strained his eyes and just managed to read the notice propped up on the tea trolley. We've magnified it so you can read it. Which cakes can Ivor eat safely?

The Family

I vor picked the stickiest looking cake and bit into it. The red jam ran down his chin. "Yum yum, terrif...", he thought, then something seemed to go wrong with his brain. The Tea lady's hideously ugly face loomed very close to his own. The ground seemed closer than it should be too . . .

The bumping, banging and rattling was making his head ache and he felt sick, but luckily the brain disease seemed to have gone away. He cautiously moved his body and found he was sitting on the tea trolley. His feet and hands were roped to the four corners of it.

A strangled grunt and a violent jolt of the trolley prompted Ivor to peer cautiously out, but all he could see

was a frightened spider, the twin of his friend in the box, scurrying down the corridor.

He stared again at the Tea Lady. Could she be one of Boris's "family" in disguise? He thought about some photographs he had once seen of them.

A sudden awful stomach-lurch told him they were in a lift – going down. "That's the one!" thought Ivor, just as his stomach settled in its right place again and the lift doors opened. "That might be useful", he thought and dozed off again.

DON'T TURN THE PAGE YET.

Here are the photographs of the family which Ivor had seen. Which of them do you think is the tea lady?

Captured!

CHANDELIER

COGS

MOUSE

PENDULUM

CHEESE SANDWICH

BOX

LEVER

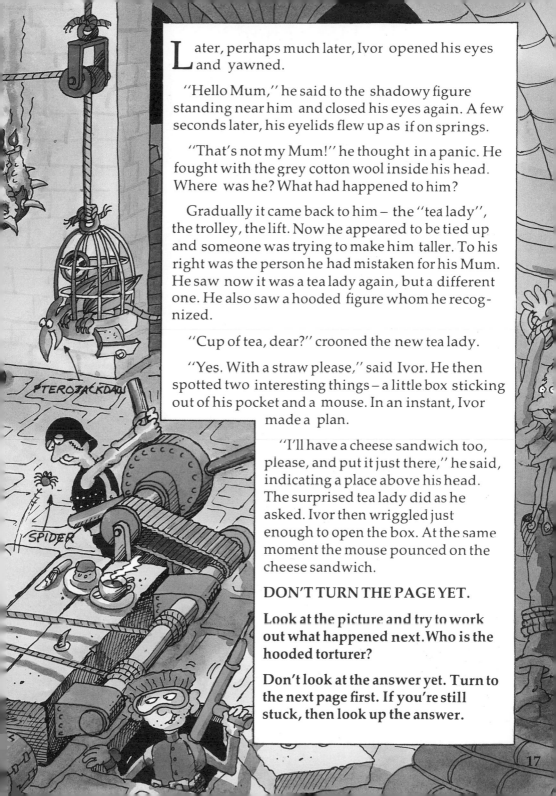

Later, perhaps much later, Ivor opened his eyes and yawned.

"Hello Mum," he said to the shadowy figure standing near him and closed his eyes again. A few seconds later, his eyelids flew up as if on springs.

"That's not my Mum!" he thought in a panic. He fought with the grey cotton wool inside his head. Where was he? What had happened to him?

Gradually it came back to him – the "tea lady", the trolley, the lift. Now he appeared to be tied up and someone was trying to make him taller. To his right was the person he had mistaken for his Mum. He saw now it was a tea lady again, but a different one. He also saw a hooded figure whom he recognized.

"Cup of tea, dear?" crooned the new tea lady.

"Yes. With a straw please," said Ivor. He then spotted two interesting things – a little box sticking out of his pocket and a mouse. In an instant, Ivor made a plan.

"I'll have a cheese sandwich too, please, and put it just there," he said, indicating a place above his head. The surprised tea lady did as he asked. Ivor then wriggled just enough to open the box. At the same moment the mouse pounced on the cheese sandwich.

DON'T TURN THE PAGE YET.

Look at the picture and try to work out what happened next. Who is the hooded torturer?

Don't look at the answer yet. Turn to the next page first. If you're still stuck, then look up the answer.

PTEROJACKDAW

SPIDER

What Really Happened?

These pictures show what happened in the dungeon during the chaos that followed the spider's escape – or do they?

Some of these things happened, but not in the order shown. Can you sort out which pictures tell the truth and in what order?

The lever pulls the trapdoor open, letting the balls through.

The mouse jumps on Roxanne's nose and she runs away.

The mouse jumps on to the sandwich, pushing the lever down.

The pterojackdaw's cage falls on Horace's head and knocks him out.

The pterojackdaw gets free and attacks Arthur.

The noose tightens round Roxanne's foot, tripping her up and knocking over the tea trolley.

The rope holding the pendulum burns and it crashes down.

Ivor wriggles up the bed and is able to unhook his handropes.

Arthur is submerged by the contents of the tea trolley.

The spider frightens Horace who lets go of the wheel, loosening Ivor's ropes.

The chandelier is winched up by the machine and the candles burn through the rope holding the cage.

Ivor adds to his "useful" things

The dungeon floor was littered with bits and pieces. Ivor couldn't resist cramming some of them into his already overloaded pockets. Here you can see what he picked up.

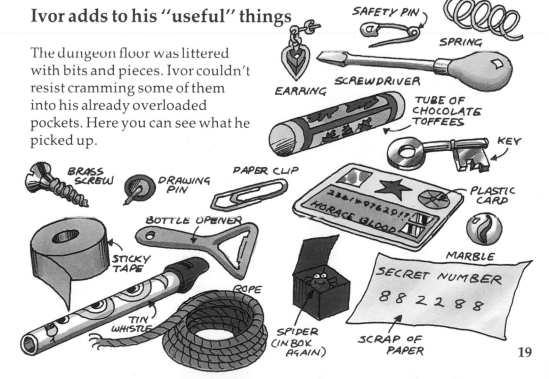

SAFETY PIN

SPRING

EARRING

SCREWDRIVER

TUBE OF CHOCOLATE TOFFEES

KEY

BRASS SCREW

DRAWING PIN

PAPER CLIP

PLASTIC CARD

2341497620!7

HORACE BLOOD

MARBLE

BOTTLE OPENER

STICKY TAPE

ROPE

TIN WHISTLE

SPIDER (IN BOX AGAIN)

SECRET NUMBER

8 8 2 2 8 8

SCRAP OF PAPER

19

Escape from the Dungeon

ROXANNE'S MUMMY

GRANDFATHER BLOOD'S BICYCLE

USED TO CONTAIN A PLANT

FRUIT MACHINE

HORACE'S DISGUISES

PEARL'S BICYCLE

SPIDER-EATING PLANT

THE MOUSE THAT HELPED IVOR ESCAPE

SLIME

I vor grabbed a sandwich from the overturned tea trolley and, with pockets and cheeks bulging, he thought about what to do next.

Obviously he must get out of the dungeon before Horace and the others came to. Then he must find the lift and the Papers. But which of the seven identical green doors should he go through?

He had been half-asleep, half-awake while the tea trolley had trundled him along. Hazy memories floated into his mind. Yes, he

AWFUL ARTHUR'S PRIZE PIRANHA

HORACE'S FRIENDS

BLOOD FAMILY COAT OF ARMS

5

6

7

POISONOUS PALM

ARTHUR'S BICYCLE

NORMAN'S BICYCLE

FRUIT MACHINE

STINGING FERN

FRUIT MACHINE

MORE OF PEARL'S EMPTIES

TO THE SEWER

UNCLE SPIKE'S LOST ROLLER SKATE

PEARL'S EMPTIES

remembered entering the dungeon now. He had passed close to a fruit machine. It was on his left . . . or was it right? He remembered the trolley's back right-hand wheel brushing past a bicycle and almost knocking it over, too. He concentrated harder and remembered something odd

hanging from the ceiling and some crates in front of the fruit machine.

DON'T TURN THE PAGE YET.

Which of the doors in the picture should Ivor go through?

21

Norman and the Pinball Machine

Having made his decision, Ivor pushed the door. It wouldn't open. He pushed again, leaning his whole weight on it, and suddenly it swung open. He stumbled through into the gloom and found himself face to chest with nephew Norman.

"Hello," said Norman. "Who are you? Come and play pinball with me."

Ivor gulped and produced what he hoped was a friendly smile. He'd never come higher than 153rd on the school pinball ladder. Norman's vice-like grip on his arm didn't encourage him to refuse and he found himself being led along the corridor.

After two left and three right turns, Norman opened a door.

"Wow!" said Ivor. The most amazing pinball machine Ivor had ever seen stood in the middle of the room. It was huge and covered with brightly coloured pictures and lights.

"My turn first," said Norman, who immediately sent the first ball whizzing round the machine. Ivor's eyes grew bigger and rounder as he watched. This boy was GOOD. He notched up a score of 208,361 with one ball!

"OK", said Norman, "now you've got to match my score exactly, or I shan't let you leave the room."

DON'T TURN THE PAGE YET.

What route should Ivor's ball take round the machine to match Norman's score?

TOP SCORER: G. BLOOD

208, 361

22

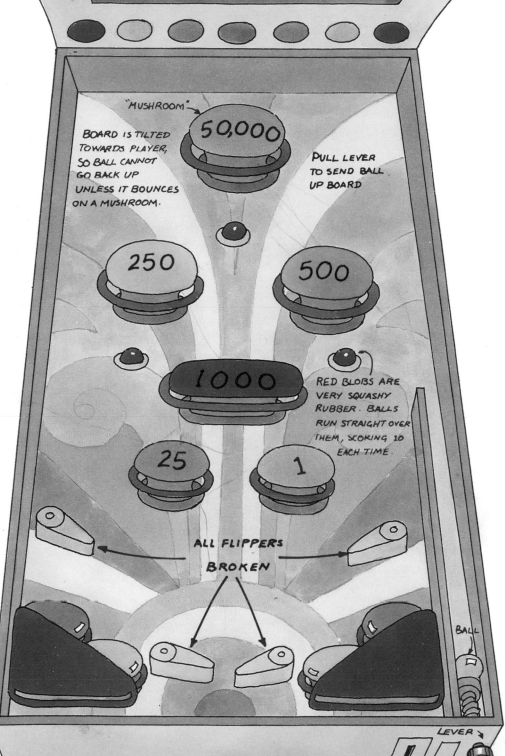

"MUSHROOM"

50,000

BOARD IS TILTED
TOWARDS PLAYER,
SO BALL CANNOT
GO BACK UP
UNLESS IT BOUNCES
ON A MUSHROOM.

PULL LEVER
TO SEND BALL
UP BOARD

250

500

1000

RED BLOBS ARE
VERY SQUASHY
RUBBER. BALLS
RUN STRAIGHT OVER
THEM, SCORING 10
EACH TIME.

25

1

ALL FLIPPERS
BROKEN

BALL

LEVER

23

The Surprising Toffees

Norman jumped up and down hysterically. "3325! You'll have to stay here for ever!"

Ivor's heart couldn't sink any further. He reached into his pocket and pulled out the tube of chocolate toffees he'd found in the torture room.

"Want one?" he said, and Norman's greedy eyes lit up. He took ten and crammed them all in his mouth at once. Disgusted, Ivor took one for himself and was on the point of putting it in his mouth, when he noticed Norman's face change. He made a strangled sound and crashed heavily to the floor.

Horrified, Ivor dropped the toffee he was holding and let the rest of the packet fall after it.

He turned to go but the walls were completely covered with shelves. There was no sign of the door. He scanned the room, searching for a clue to the way out. The cursor on the computer screen winked at him.

"Which way?" it asked. Ivor felt like kicking it. He pressed some keys and got a picture on the screen.

"Oh, I see," he said.

DON'T TURN THE PAGE YET.

What did Ivor do next?

TOP SCORER: G. BLOOD

208/351

CHOCOLATE TOFFEES

USEFUL THINGS

BORIS'S FOOT

PIRANHA BIRD

NORM

DIRTY WASHING

WHICH WAY?DOWN

COMPUTER GAMES
DIY
ECONOMICS
PINBALL HEROES

OLD RUG

25

Blood Castle Underground

Ivor squeezed through the hole and found himself in a twisty passage. Somehow or other he must find his way to the lift and get back upstairs. **DON'T TURN THE PAGE YET.**

Work out where Ivor is and which route he should take to the lift.

(NOTE: SOME OF THE PASSAGES GO BEHIND OTHERS — YOU ARE ALLOWED TO GO ALONG THESE.)

PORTRAITS OF BORIS CONCEAL TV CAMERAS — AVOID THEM.

AWFUL ARTHUR'S PRACTICE TANK

SHARK

BORIS →

NEPHEW NORMAN

TRAP DOOR

TRAP-DOOR IN FLOOR

BORIS

SLIPPERY SHAFT

SHARP SPIKES

PAULINE

PEARL'S HIDEAWAY

ROXANNE'S MAKE-UP ROOM

SNAKE PIT

WAY OUT

BORIS →

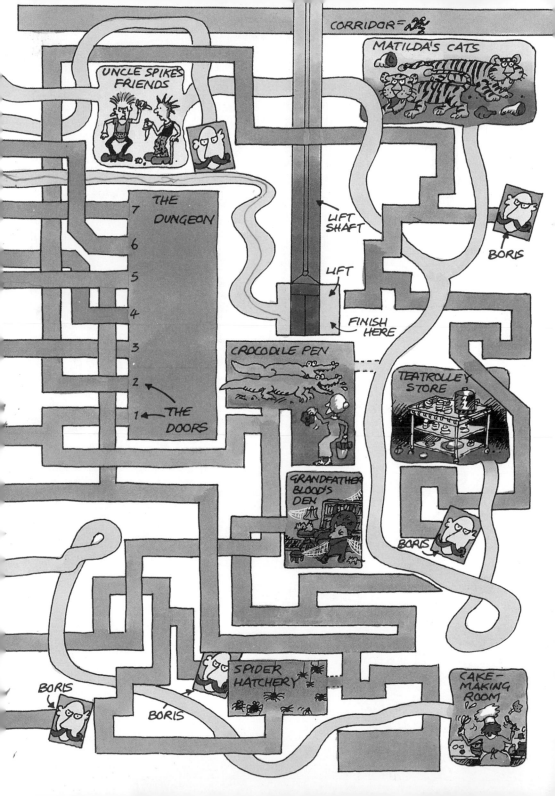

Ivor Goes Up

At last Ivor found himself standing in front of a lift. He stepped inside and the door closed behind him. The control panel looked like an aeroplane flight deck and was so high up Ivor had to stand on tip-toe to see it. There were flashing coloured lights, digital displays, dials and gauges, and a set of buttons numbered from zero to nine. Ivor did some calculations and decided which button to press.

Nothing happened. On closer examination, he realized that the buttons were shielded by a layer of clear perspex.

?

Ivor stared thoughtfully at the panel. He then started poking at it with something he found in his pocket. Ah! Something was happening. The perspex panel slid across to expose the buttons, so Ivor pressed some of them and, at last, the lift set off upwards.

A voice in his ear made Ivor jump higher than the control panel. It seemed to be coming from the portrait of Boris hanging on the wall.

"He's escaped. Guard the East Turret immediately. Repeat. Guard the East Turret."

"Gosh," thought Ivor, "They must think I'm Horace!"

The lift stopped as suddenly as it had started, the doors slid open and Ivor stepped out.

DON'T TURN THE PAGE YET.

How did Ivor make the lift work and why did "they" think he was Horace?

SPIKE

On the Roof

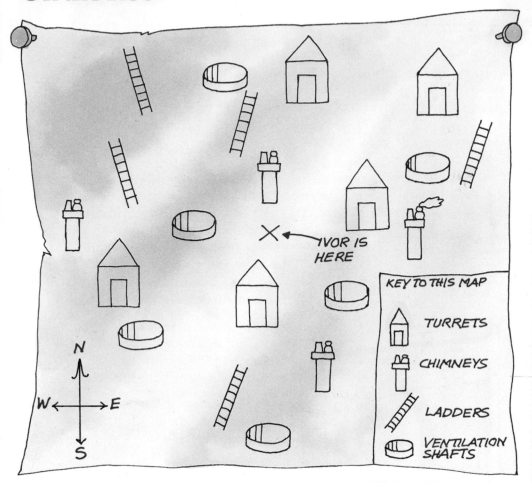

IVOR IS HERE

KEY TO THIS MAP

TURRETS

CHIMNEYS

LADDERS

VENTILATION SHAFTS

A cold wind hit Ivor in the face. He was outdoors! He walked to the nearest wall, leaned over and pulled sharply back. He was an awfully long way from the ground.

Ivor threaded his way through the ventilation shafts and chimneys. He was wondering where to go next when he came across a map.

"If they are so keen on guarding the east turret," he thought, "there must be something of interest there. It must be that one . . . or that one. Hmmm, which direction is east?"

DON'T TURN THE PAGE YET.

Above you can see the map Ivor is looking at and, on the right, the roofscape views (not in order) he sees by turning through 90° at a time. What is the colour of the door on the east turret?

What the Papers Say

Ivor kicked open the brightly painted door like people do in gangster films and waited to see what would happen.

"Stick 'em up!" screamed a harsh voice and Ivor did so, terrified.

"Stick 'em up! Steeck 'emm uppp! Steeeeeck 'emmmmmmmmmmm upppppppppppppppppp! Whirr clank."

Ivor pushed the door again. Silence. There was no-one in sight. He went in, almost tripping over an ancient tape recorder and the deep carpet. Expensive-looking paintings hung on the walls. There was certainly something of interest here. He glanced through an open door and saw a sumptuously furnished office, complete with antique desk.

The room was empty, so Ivor tip-

TESTAMENT

OKER TABLE, MY

VER SAFETY PINS

SON SPIKE, MY

MY DIVING

ON TO ART

ANTIQUE SIL

BOXES TO MY

LEG TO HERBERT

HARPOON COLLECTI

HA BIRD AND MY

TO BABY NORMAN

F THE CROCODILE AN

TO MATILDA AN

STRET

THIS IS

OF GRA

I HEREB

COLLECTION

AND MY JUKE

WOODEN

GEAR AND

MY PIRAN

MACHINE

COPIES

MONTHL

ENT

toed in. Perhaps the Papers would be here – they would surely have been moved from their original hiding place by now. He searched the desk drawers but found nothing. He glanced around the room but all he could see was a very dirty, dog-eared envelope which had fallen on the floor. He picked it up and looked inside. All it contained was torn scraps of paper. He tipped them out on to the desk, idly wondering what they could be.

Then a few words caught his eye: "Last will . . . Blood . . . wealth . . . ." and he frantically started putting together this paper jigsaw puzzle.

DON'T TURN THE PAGE YET.

What do the scraps of paper say?

Ivor Meets Boris

Ivor's brain hurt . . . and his heart too. This wasn't what he'd expected to find! He stuffed the scraps back into the envelope, pushed it into his pocket and turned to leave the room.

There, outlined in the doorway, was Boris.

Ivor wasn't even scared any more. He was too disheartened to care what happened next. He stared coolly at the tall, still figure.

What did happen next surprised him. He heard his own voice cry out.

"You're not Boris!" it said.

DON'T TURN THE PAGE YET.

How did Ivor know that the man in front of him was not Boris?

BORIS: A STUDY OF HANDS

MY EAR BY ARTHUR

ROXANNE

Spike was here

THE DESK

THE TWINS AT PLAY

34

The Prisoner

Ivor darted for the door and slipped past Boris's legs before Boris had time to close his mouth. Down the corridor, up some steps and through a door sped Ivor. He waited breathing heavily. There was no sign that he had been followed.

The room was very gloomy.

BORIS BY MATILDA

He could hardly see anything at all, but he could hear some faint sounds coming from somewhere to his left. He found a door. The noises were definitely coming from the other side of it.

The door was stiff and creaky but there was more light on the other side. Ivor couldn't believe his eyes. There, inside a gigantic cage, was Boris! A few seconds' thought led Ivor to the conclusion that it must be the real Boris, his genuine cousin.

"Ivor! How pleased I am to see you!" said Boris.

Ivor didn't reply. He was still suspicious of Boris, real or not.

"I've been a prisoner here since Grandfather Blood died and Wicked Wilf came back from Australia and started impersonating me. You've got to help me to escape."

"OK," Ivor said, after a while. "I've got an idea. Hand me that rope."

Ivor then proceeded to free Boris from his cage.

DON'T TURN THE PAGE YET.

What did Ivor do to release Boris from the cage?

The Escape Plan

A scrap of paper on the floor caught Ivor's eye. He picked it up. This is it:

GRANDSON IVOR, PROVIDING MY DAUGHTER MATILDA IS STILL ALIVE AND MY

"What's that?" asked Boris. Ivor showed him and the rest of the pieces he'd found in the envelope.

"The Will! We've no time to lose! We must find Aunt Matilda and get out of Blood Castle as soon as possible, so we can claim our inheritances. I bet I can guess where she'll be and, what's more, I know how we can escape!"

"How?" said Ivor, disbelievingly.

"Easy! Grandfather Blood gave me this just before he died. Thank goodness I can read music! You must have seen Aunt Matilda somewhere in the castle. Think carefully."

DON'T TURN THE PAGE YET.

This is what Grandfather Blood gave Boris. How can they use it to help them escape? (You don't have to be able to read music to work it out.) Where did they find Aunt Matilda?

The Truth at Last

Boris's plan worked like a charm. Aunt Matilda was where Ivor had seen her earlier and the three of them made their escape, using Grandfather Blood's music and Ivor's tin whistle.

As they stood outside breathing the fresh air, Ivor realized they were not a stone's throw from where he had started, goodness knows how long ago. Quickly and quietly they made their way through the gate and up the tree-lined road beyond it. When they reached the top of the hill, they paused to look back. They saw the dim shapes of "Boris", Herbert and Horace loading suitcases into Grandfather Blood's battered old Rolls Royce.

"They're running away!" cried Ivor.

"Let them", said Boris. "They won't get far."

They watched while the ancient Rolls chugged through the gate and out of sight. An hour later, tired and breathless, they reached the home of Mr Sprog, the Blood family's lawyer.

Mrs Sprog produced a wonderful tea for them, which they attacked gratefully while they told Mr Sprog their story. After a while, Ivor looked at Boris thoughtfully and said, "I don't understand how you came to have the scrap of the Will which mentioned me."

Boris explained that Wicked Wilf had torn this piece off himself and that he, Boris, had managed to hide it and keep it safe.

"But", said Boris, "What I don't understand is what would have happened to the legacy if Aunt Matilda were not still alive?"

They all looked at Aunt Matilda, who had turned slightly pink.

"Oh well", she said, and produced a scrap of paper from her handbag. This is what it said:

" . . . otherwise everything is to go to World Spider Sanctuary."

She explained her worry that Pearl's passion for spiders might make her do something dangerous.

"Well, there's only one question left," said Mr Sprog. "Who tore up the Will?"

They all looked blankly at each other.

Do you know?

Clues

41

Answers

Pages 4-5

Ivor notices a key on the window ledge. He climbs up by the route shown and sits on the ledge above the window. He uses the nylon thread and sharp hook from his pocket to make a fishing line and "fishes" for the key. He then climbs down by the same route, unlocks the front door and goes in.

(Did you think you could go in through the open door? This isn't a good idea – the backwards writing on this door says "SNAKE PIT".)

Ivor sits here to fish for key.

Key

Ivor climbs up this way.

Pages 6-7

Here you can see the route Ivor takes and the room he goes to.

Areas of "temporary smoothness" are these doors.

Shaft of light comes from this window.

Ivor stops to read map here.

Ivor starts here (at front door).

He feels his way with his left hand.

This is the room Ivor goes to.

Pages 8-9

The book titles are all written backwards. The second book from the right on the bottom shelf reads "HANDLE PULL HERE". He pulls it and the bookcase opens revealing the room beyond. (Try decoding the other titles – they may give you some ideas about things that happen later.)

Pages 10-11

Ivor spots that the arrows on the stairs go in different directions and that the new map shows more of the west outside wall. He concludes that his map shows the wrong floor and he needs to search the equivalent room upstairs. He makes for the nearest stairs following the route shown*. Did you find all the other differences too? They are ringed here.

Ivor starts in this room (downstairs).

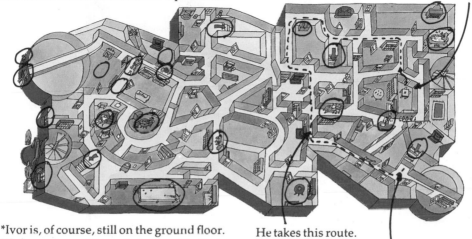

*Ivor is, of course, still on the ground floor. We have shown the route here on the first floor map, but the route on the ground floor is exactly the same.

He takes this route.

He comes up these stairs.

Pages 12-13

You can see here which cakes Ivor can eat safely.

Jam cakes contain sleeping pills.

Nut cakes are not OK.

Ivor can eat the ones without nuts.

He can eat the ones with cherries.

He can't eat this one because it's yellow.

Blue icing contains strychnine.

He can eat the pink, green and white cakes.

Pink surprises are OK.

He can't eat these because they might have lead shot in them.

Pages 14-15

The "tea lady" is Horace. The strands of red hair give him away. The Pearl "look-alike" wig hides his scar.

Pages 16-17

Here you can see what happens in the dungeon. The hooded torturer is Horace. His scar is the clue.

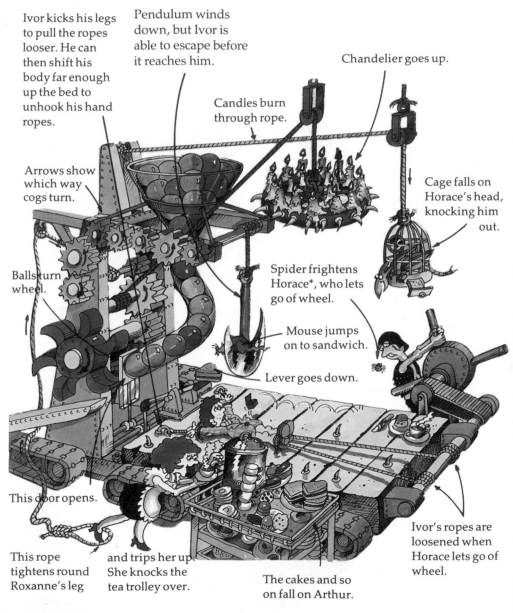

Ivor kicks his legs to pull the ropes looser. He can then shift his body far enough up the bed to unhook his hand ropes.

Pendulum winds down, but Ivor is able to escape before it reaches him.

Chandelier goes up.

Candles burn through rope.

Cage falls on Horace's head, knocking him out.

Arrows show which way cogs turn.

Spider frightens Horace*, who lets go of wheel.

Balls turn wheel.

Mouse jumps on to sandwich.

Lever goes down.

This door opens.

Ivor's ropes are loosened when Horace lets go of wheel.

This rope tightens round Roxanne's leg

and trips her up. She knocks the tea trolley over.

The cakes and so on fall on Arthur.

44 *You know Horace is frightened of spiders from page 15.

Pages 18-19

The pictures go in this order: 3, 10, 1, 6, 11, 4, 9, 8.
Pictures 2, 5 and 7 did not happen. The pendulum comes
down (follow the cogs round to see why) but Ivor has
already escaped.

Pages 20-21

The only door which fits the description completely is door 5.

Pages 22-23

This is the route Norman's ball took.

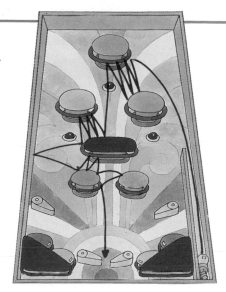

Pages 24-25

Ivor spots that Nephew Norman has a book
on computer games. When he sees the
question "WHICH WAY" on the screen, he
decides to try typing in directions, as you
would if playing a computer adventure
game. When he types "DOWN", a diagram
comes up on the screen. Ivor realizes that
this corresponds to a floor plan of the room
he is in.

Ivor then lifts the rug and finds the
trapdoor, which he opens by pulling the
ring.

(Perhaps you can work out the route
Ivor's ball took on the pinball machine.)

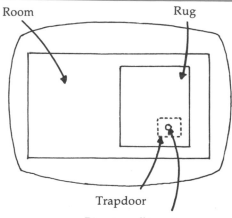

Room

Rug

Trapdoor

Ring to pull trapdoor open.

—— Ivor's route from the dungeon to Norman's room.

- - - - Ivor follows this route from Norman's room to the lift.

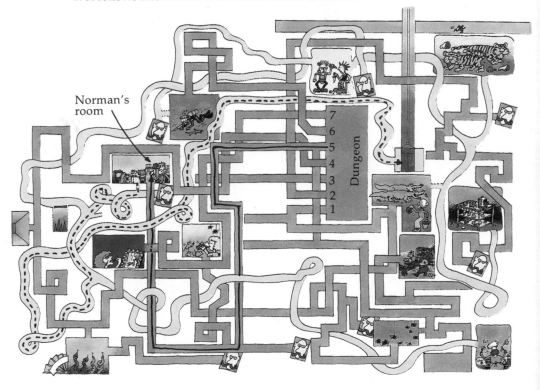

Norman's room

Dungeon

7 6 5 4 3 2 1

Pages 28-29

Ivor puts the "credit card" he found in the dungeon (see page 19) into the slot and presses the numbers written on the scrap of paper he found with it. This makes the lift work. "They" think he is Horace because the card is in Horace's name.

Pages 30-31

The east turret door is blue. (If you turn the page round so you can look at the map in the direction of east, you will see the view more clearly.)

Pages 32-33

Here is the pieced together Will:

THE WILL

THIS IS THE LAST WILL AND TESTAMENT OF GRANDFATHER BLOOD I HEREBY LEAVE MY SNOOKER TABLE, MY COLLECTION OF ANTIQUE SILVER SAFETY PINS AND MY JUKE BOXES TO MY SON SPIKE, MY WOODEN LEG TO HERBERT, MY DIVING GEAR AND HARPOON COLLECTION TO ARTHUR, MY PIRANHA BIRD AND MY PINBALL MACHINE TO BABY NORMAN, THE BOUND COPIES OF 'THE CROCODILE' AND 'SPIDER KEEPER'S MONTHLY' TO MATILDA AND PEARL, MY PATENT STRETCHER TO THE LOCAL HOSPITAL AND MY HOME KNOWN TO ALL AS BLOOD CASTLE, ALL MY WORLDLY WEALTH AND MY EXOTIC SNAKE COLLECTION TO MY GRANDSON BORIS

Pages 34-35

Ivor had seen several portraits of Boris on his travels through the castle, including one in the room he is now standing in. He notices a number of differences between these and the phoney Boris standing in the doorway. The differences are ringed on this picture.

Pages 36-37

Ivor props the ladder up against the beam, threads the rope over the pulley and hooks it on to the ring of the cage. He then threads the rope through the ring again and back over the pulley. He then climbs down and pulls on the rope.

The greasiness of the ring helps to reduce the friction between it and the rope. He is just able to pull the cage up enough for Boris to crawl out. He could have threaded the rope through the ring and over the pulley a third time. In theory this would have made the cage easier to lift. However, he was worried about there being too much friction caused by the rope rubbing against itself.

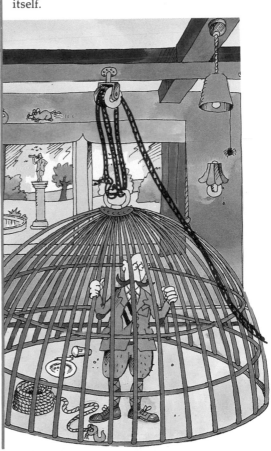

Ivor spotted Aunt Matilda with the crocodiles while he was looking for the lift (see page 27). He and Boris go back there to find her. (Ivor still has the card and number for operating the lift.)

They then make their way to the snake pit. They use the tin whistle Ivor found in the dungeon (page 19) to play Grandfather Blood's Little Tune to charm the snakes so they can get past them safely. (Clues to this are the pictures on the music, Boris's picture "thoughts" on page 38 and the book on "Snake Charming for Beginners" on page 8. Ivor remembers seeing the snake pit entrance when he was standing outside the castle trying to get in (pages 4-5).

Page 40

On page 13 there is a picture of Uncle Spike on the wall, tearing up some paper. If you look carefully, you will see the words on it are "The Will" in mirror writing, i.e. it is not a portrait, but a reflection in a mirror. So Uncle Spike tore up the Will.

You are probably wondering why. Well, not realizing Boris was an imposter and disgusted by his behaviour after Grandfather Blood's death, Spike thought he would destroy the Will and then try to get rid of Boris. However, you were not the only one to see him doing it. "Boris" saw him too, stole the pieces and took them to his turret room where Ivor found them.